To Linda,
the Renaissance woman

*First Edition, 1981*
*Published by Philomel Books*
*a division of The Putnam Publishing Group*
*200 Madison Avenue, New York, N.Y. 10016*

*No part of this publication may be reproduced,*
*stored in a retrieval system, or transmitted, in any form or by any means,*
*without prior written permission of the publisher.*

*Information on last page of this book constitutes an extension of the copyright page.*
*ISBN 0-399-20812-7*
*Designed by Sallie Baldwin/Antler & Baldwin Studio, Inc.*

All the flowers and herbs that appear in the illustrations in this volume were painted from life, as they appeared during the round of the year's seasons in Tasha Tudor's own garden. Among others, flower lovers may identify the following:

**ON ENDPAPERS:**

*Artemisia*
*Campanula glomerata*
Feverfew (*Chrysanthemum parthenium*)
*Gypsophyla paniculata*
*Geranium Alpha*
Miniature rose
Maiden's blush rose (Cuisse de nymphe)
Bloomfield Dainty (a musk rose)
*Viola tricola* (Ladies' Delight)
Hidcote Beauty (a *Fuchsia*)
*Malva* (mallow)
Forget-me-not

**ON DEDICATION PAGE:**

Bloomfield Dainty rose

**ON TITLE PAGE:**

Rosemary
*Rosa nitida*
*Campanula*

**JANUARY:**

Seed pods of *rosa multiflora*
Seed pods of *pinxter* bush (Azalea)
Seed pods of Sensitive fern
Seed pods of black-eyed Susan
Dried goldenrod

**FEBRUARY:**

Violet
Forget-me-not
*Convallaria majalis* (lily-of-the-valley)
Moss rose
Ivy
Bleeding heart
Hay fern
*Fuschia*

**MARCH:**

Pussywillows
Birch catkins
Fern fronds
Skunk cabbage

**APRIL:**

Pussywillow catkins
Birch catkins
*Narcissus poeticus*

**MAY:**

*Primula vulgaris*
Keys of Heaven (a *Primula*)
Daffodils
Bloodroot
Fiddleheads of Interrupted fern

**JUNE:**

*Rosa soulianna*
*Delphinium*
Regal lily
*Gypsophyla*
Interrupted fern
Shrub roses
Crested moss rose
    (Chapeau de Napoleon)
Maidenhair fern

**JULY:**

Koenigen von Daenemarck
    (Queen of Denmark) rose
*Geranium* "tree"
Old shrub rose

**AUGUST:**

*Artemisia*
Crane's-bill (*Geranium*)
*Valeriana*
Lilies, various
Lettuce poppies
Hollyhocks

**SEPTEMBER:**

Witch hazel blooms and pods
New England aster
Woodbine leaves and berries

**OCTOBER:**

Apples
Goldenrod
New England aster

**NOVEMBER:**

Interrupted fern
Bittersweet
British Soldier
Fairy cups

**DECEMBER:**

Oats
Wheat

# ROSEMARY FOR REMEMBRANCE

## A Keepsake Book
## TASHA TUDOR

PHILOMEL BOOKS
*New York*

There is no Frigate like a Book
To take us Lands away
Nor any Coursers like a Page
Of prancing Poetry—
This Traverse may the poorest take
Without oppress of Toll—
How frugal is the Chariot
That bears the Human Soul.

EMILY DICKINSON

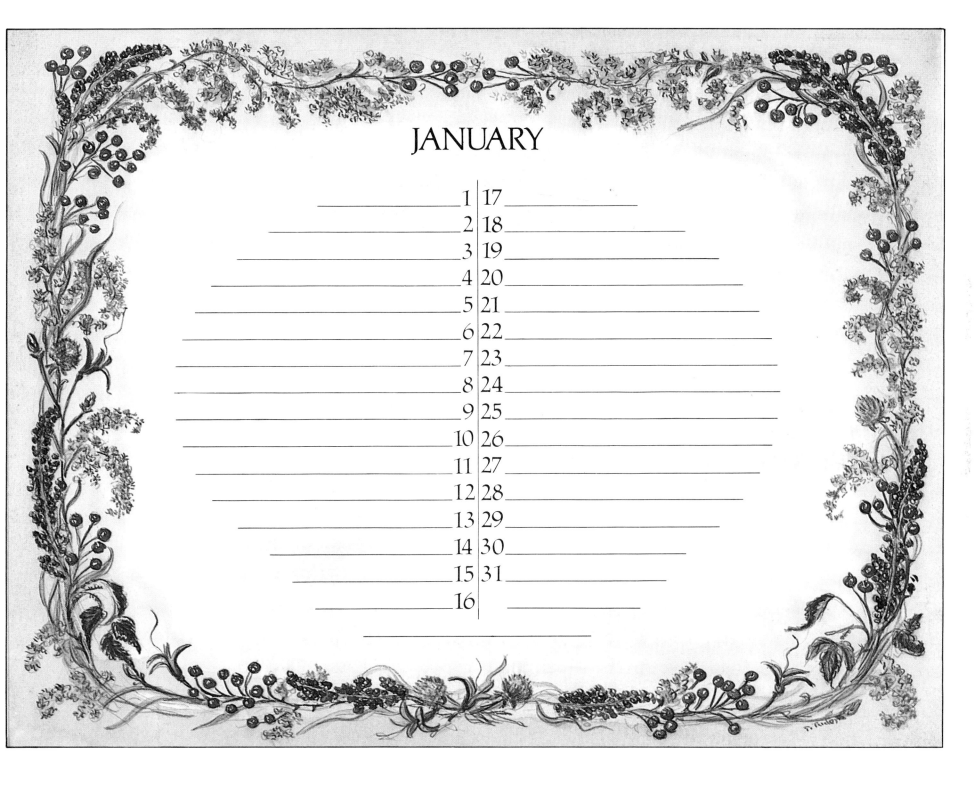

# JANUARY

| | |
|---|---|
| _____ 1 | 17 _____ |
| _____ 2 | 18 _____ |
| _____ 3 | 19 _____ |
| _____ 4 | 20 _____ |
| _____ 5 | 21 _____ |
| _____ 6 | 22 _____ |
| _____ 7 | 23 _____ |
| _____ 8 | 24 _____ |
| _____ 9 | 25 _____ |
| _____ 10 | 26 _____ |
| _____ 11 | 27 _____ |
| _____ 12 | 28 _____ |
| _____ 13 | 29 _____ |
| _____ 14 | 30 _____ |
| _____ 15 | 31 _____ |
| _____ 16 | _____ |

My true love hath my heart and I have his
    By just exchange—one for the other given!
I hold his dear and mine he cannot miss,
    There never was a better bargain driven—
My true love hath my heart and I have his.

SIR PHILIP SYDNEY

# FEBRUARY

| | |
|---|---|
| 1 | 16 |
| 2 | 17 |
| 3 | 18 |
| 4 | 19 |
| 5 | 20 |
| 6 | 21 |
| 7 | 22 |
| 8 | 23 |
| 9 | 24 |
| 10 | 25 |
| 11 | 26 |
| 12 | 27 |
| 13 | 28 |
| 14 | 29 |
| 15 | |

How fading are the joys we dote upon!
Like apparitions seen and gone.
But those that soonest take their flight
Are those most exquisite and strong—
Like angels' visits, short and bright,
Mortality's too weak to bear them long.

JOHN NORRIS

# MARCH

| | |
|---|---|
| 1 | 17 |
| 2 | 18 |
| 3 | 19 |
| 4 | 20 |
| 5 | 21 |
| 6 | 22 |
| 7 | 23 |
| 8 | 24 |
| 9 | 25 |
| 10 | 26 |
| 11 | 27 |
| 12 | 28 |
| 13 | 29 |
| 14 | 30 |
| 15 | 31 |
| 16 | |

*And pluck till time and times are done*
*The silver apples of the moon.*
*The golden apples of the sun.*

WILLIAM BUTLER YEATS

# APRIL

| | |
|---|---|
| _____ 1 | 16 _____ |
| _____ 2 | 17 _____ |
| _____ 3 | 18 _____ |
| _____ 4 | 19 _____ |
| _____ 5 | 20 _____ |
| _____ 6 | 21 _____ |
| _____ 7 | 22 _____ |
| _____ 8 | 23 _____ |
| _____ 9 | 24 _____ |
| _____ 10 | 25 _____ |
| _____ 11 | 26 _____ |
| _____ 12 | 27 _____ |
| _____ 13 | 28 _____ |
| _____ 14 | 29 _____ |
| _____ 15 | 30 _____ |

_____

*Grief can take care of itself, but to get the full value of joy you must have somebody to divide it with.*

MARK TWAIN

# MAY

1 | 17
2 | 18
3 | 19
4 | 20
5 | 21
6 | 22
7 | 23
8 | 24
9 | 25
10 | 26
11 | 27
12 | 28
13 | 29
14 | 30
15 | 31
16 |

The innocent and the beautiful
Have no enemy but time.

WILLIAM BUTLER YEATS

# JUNE

| | |
|---|---|
| 1 | 16 |
| 2 | 17 |
| 3 | 18 |
| 4 | 19 |
| 5 | 20 |
| 6 | 21 |
| 7 | 22 |
| 8 | 23 |
| 9 | 24 |
| 10 | 25 |
| 11 | 26 |
| 12 | 27 |
| 13 | 28 |
| 14 | 29 |
| 15 | 30 |

*Be secret and exult,*
*Because of all things*
*known*
*That is most diffiult.*

WILLIAM BUTLER YEATS

# JULY

| | |
|---|---|
| 1 | 17 |
| 2 | 18 |
| 3 | 19 |
| 4 | 20 |
| 5 | 21 |
| 6 | 22 |
| 7 | 23 |
| 8 | 24 |
| 9 | 25 |
| 10 | 26 |
| 11 | 27 |
| 12 | 28 |
| 13 | 29 |
| 14 | 30 |
| 15 | 31 |
| 16 | |

Though we travel the world over to find the beautiful we must carry it with us or we find it not.

RALPH WALDO EMERSON

# AUGUST

1 | 17
2 | 18
3 | 19
4 | 20
5 | 21
6 | 22
7 | 23
8 | 24
9 | 25
10 | 26
11 | 27
12 | 28
13 | 29
14 | 30
15 | 31
16 |

For the animals shall not be measured by man. In a world older and more complete than ours they move finished and complete, gifted with extensions of the senses we have lost or never attained, living by voices we shall never hear. They are not brethren, they are not underlings, they are other nations, caught with ourselves in the net of life and time, fellow prisoners of the splendour and travail of the earth.

HENRY BOSTON

# SEPTEMBER

| | |
|---|---|
| _____ 1 | 16 _____ |
| _____ 2 | 17 _____ |
| _____ 3 | 18 _____ |
| _____ 4 | 19 _____ |
| _____ 5 | 20 _____ |
| _____ 6 | 21 _____ |
| _____ 7 | 22 _____ |
| _____ 8 | 23 _____ |
| _____ 9 | 24 _____ |
| _____ 10 | 25 _____ |
| _____ 11 | 26 _____ |
| _____ 12 | 27 _____ |
| _____ 13 | 28 _____ |
| _____ 14 | 29 _____ |
| _____ 15 | 30 _____ |

_____

Season of mists and mellow
  fruitfulness!
Close bosom-friend of the
  maturing sun;
Conspiring with him how to
  load and bless
With fruit the vines that round
  the thatch eaves run.
  JOHN KEATS

# OCTOBER

1 | 17
2 | 18
3 | 19
4 | 20
5 | 21
6 | 22
7 | 23
8 | 24
9 | 25
10 | 26
11 | 27
12 | 28
13 | 29
14 | 30
15 | 31
16

When love and skill
work together, expect
a masterpiece.

JOHN RUSKIN

# NOVEMBER

| | |
|---|---|
| _____ 1 | 16 _____ |
| _____ 2 | 17 _____ |
| _____ 3 | 18 _____ |
| _____ 4 | 19 _____ |
| _____ 5 | 20 _____ |
| _____ 6 | 21 _____ |
| _____ 7 | 22 _____ |
| _____ 8 | 23 _____ |
| _____ 9 | 24 _____ |
| _____ 10 | 25 _____ |
| _____ 11 | 26 _____ |
| _____ 12 | 27 _____ |
| _____ 13 | 28 _____ |
| _____ 14 | 29 _____ |
| _____ 15 | 30 _____ |

_____

The gloom of the world is but a shadow;
behind it, yet within our reach is joy.
Take joy.

FRA GIOVANNI

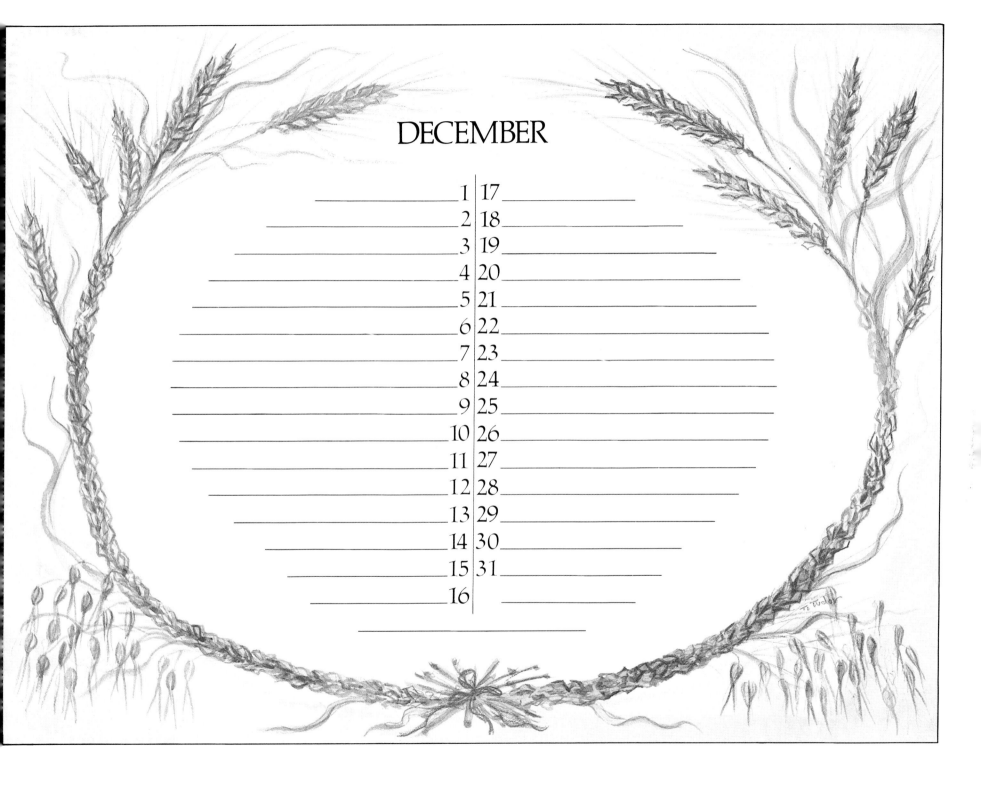

# DECEMBER

1   17
2   18
3   19
4   20
5   21
6   22
7   23
8   24
9   25
10   26
11   27
12   28
13   29
14   30
15   31
16

Tasha Tudor and Philomel Books gratefully thank the following authors and publishers whose interest, cooperation and permission to reprint have made possible the preparation of this volume. All possible care has been taken to trace the ownership of every selection included and to make full acknowledgment for its use. If any errors have accidentally occurred, they will be corrected in subsequent editions, provided notification is sent to the publishers.

Holt, Rinehart and Winston, New York, for lines from (September) *Outermost House* by Henry Boston, copyright © 1928 by Holt, Rinehart and Winston. M.B. Yeats, Anne Yeats, and Macmillan Publishers Ltd., London; and Macmillan Publishing Company, Inc. New York, for lines from the following poems by William Butler Yeats: (April) *The Song of the Wandering Aengus;* (June) *In Memory of Eva Gore-Booth and Con Markiewicz;* and (July) *To a Friend Whose Work Has Come to Nothing,* copyright © 1916, 1933 by Macmillan Publishing Company Inc., renewed 1944, 1961 by Bertha Georgie Yeats.